SACRAMENTO PUBLIC LIBRARY

D0464689

Dear Parent:
Your child's love of reading starts here!

Every child learns to read in a different way and at his or her own speed. Some go back and forth between reading levels and read favorite books again and again. Others read through each level in order. You can help your young reader improve and become more confident by encouraging his or her own interests and abilities. From books your child reads with you to the first books he or she reads alone, there are I Can Read Books for every stage of reading:

SHARED READING
Basic language, word repetition, and whimsical illustrations, ideal for sharing with your emergent reader

BEGINNING READING
Short sentences, familiar words, and simple concepts for children eager to read on their own

READING WITH HELP
Engaging stories, longer sentences, and language play for developing readers

READING ALONE
Complex plots, challenging vocabulary, and high-interest topics for the independent reader

ADVANCED READING
Short paragraphs, chapters, and exciting themes for the perfect bridge to chapter books

I Can Read Books have introduced children to the joy of reading since 1957. Featuring award-winning authors and illustrators and a fabulous cast of beloved characters, I Can Read Books set the standard for beginning readers.

A lifetime of discovery begins with the magical words **"I Can Read!"**

Visit www.icanread.com for information
on enriching your child's reading experience.

for Julia,
who likes to practice
with a string bean
when she can

HarperCollins®, 📖®, and I Can Read Book® are trademarks of HarperCollins Publishers.

Bread and Jam for Frances Text copyright © 1964 by Russell C. Hoban; renewed 1992 by Russell C. Hoban Illustrations copyright © 1964,
by Lillian Hoban; renewed 1992 by Lillian Hoban Abridged edition copyright © 2008 Russell Hoban and the Estate of Lillian Hoban All r
reserved. Printed in the United States of America. No part of this book may be used or reproduced in any manner whatsoever without wr
permission except in the case of brief quotations embodied in critical articles and reviews. For information address HarperCollins Child
Books, a division of HarperCollins Publishers, 1350 Avenue of the Americas, New York, NY 10019. www.harpercollinschildrens.com

Library of Congress Cataloging-in-Publication Data is available.
ISBN 978-0-06-083798-3 (trade bdg.) — ISBN 978-0-06-083800-3 (pbk.)

❖

I Can Read!™

REApING 2 WITH HELP

BREAD AND JAM FOR FRANCES

by Russell Hoban
Pictures by Lillian Hoban

HarperCollinsPublishers

It was breakfast time.

Father was eating his egg.

Mother was eating her egg.

Gloria was sitting in a high chair
and eating her egg too.

Frances was eating bread and jam.

"What a lovely egg!" said Father.

"It is just the thing to start the day
off right," said Mother.

Frances did not eat her egg.

Frances sang a little song to it.

She sang the song very softly:

> *I do not like the way you slide,*
>
> *I do not like your soft inside,*
>
> *I do not like you lots of ways,*
>
> *And I could do for many days*
>
> *Without eggs.*

Frances spread jam

on another slice of bread.

"Why do you keep eating
bread and jam," asked Father,
"when you have a lovely egg?"
"I like bread and jam," said Frances,
"because it does not slide off
your spoon in a funny way."

"Well, of course," said Father.

"But there are other kinds of eggs."

"Yes," said Frances.

"But sunny-side-up eggs

lie on the plate and look up at you.

And sunny-side-down eggs

just lie on their stomachs and *wait*."

13

"I think it is time for you
to go to school now," said Mother.

rances picked up her books,

er lunch box, and her skipping rope.

hen she kissed Mother and Father

ood-bye and went to the bus stop.

While she waited for the bus
she skipped and sang:

Jam on biscuits, jam on toast,

Jam is the thing that I like most.

Jam is sticky, jam is sweet,

Jam is tasty, jam's a treat—

Rasp*berry,* straw*berry,* goose*berry,*

I'm *very*

FOND . . . OF . . . JAM!

hat evening for dinner

other cooked breaded veal cutlets,

ith string beans and baked potatoes.

h!" said Father. "What is there

cer on the plate and tastier to eat

an breaded veal cutlet!"

t *is* a nice dish," said Mother.

at up the string bean, Gloria."

rances looked at her plate and sang:

> *What do cutlets wear*
>
> *Before they're breaded?*
>
> *Flannel nightgowns? Cowboy boots?*
>
> *Furry jackets? Sailor suits?*

19

Then Frances spread jam

on a slice of bread and took a bite.

"She won't try *anything* new,"

said Mother to Father.

"Well," said Frances,

"there are many different

things to eat,

and they taste many different ways.

But when I have bread and jam

I always know what I am getting,

and I am always pleased."

"You try new things

in your school lunches," said Mother.

"Today I gave you

a chicken-salad sandwich."

"I traded it to Albert," said Frances.

"For what?" said Father.

"Bread and jam," said Frances.

he next morning at breakfast

ather sat down and said,

Now I call that a pretty sight!

resh orange juice

nd poached eggs on toast."

rances began to sing a little song:

> *Poached eggs on toast,*
>
> *Why do you shiver*
>
> *With such a funny little quiver?*

hen she looked down and saw

at she did not have a poached egg.

"I have no poached egg," said Frances.

"I have nothing but orange juice."

"I know," said Mother.

"Why is that?" said Frances.

"Even Gloria has a poached egg,

and she is nothing but a baby."

24

"You do not like eggs," said Mother.

"Have some bread and jam

if you are hungry."

So Frances ate bread and jam

and went to school.

When the lunch bell rang

Frances sat down next to her friend Albe

"What do you have today?" said Frances

"I have a cream cheese-cucumber-

and-tomato sandwich," said Albert.

"And a hard-boiled egg and salt shaker.

And a thermos of milk.

And a bunch of grapes.

And a tangerine and a cup custard.

What do you have?" he said.

Frances opened her lunch.

"Bread and jam," she said.

"You're lucky," said Albert.

"That's just what you like."

"I had bread and jam

for dinner last night," said Frances,

"and for breakfast this morning.

I am a very lucky girl, I guess."

Albert took a napkin

and tucked it under his chin.

He arranged his lunch neatly.

"I *like* cream cheese with cucumber

and tomatoes on rye," said Albert.

With his spoon he cracked the egg.

He sprinkled salt on the yolk.

He took a bite of sandwich,

a bite of egg, and a drink of milk.

Then he went around again.

Albert made the sandwich,

the egg, and the milk come out even.

Albert sighed. "I like to have
a good lunch," he said.

Frances ate her bread and jam.

Then she went out to the playground

and skipped rope.

She did not skip as fast

as she had skipped in the morning,

and she sang:

Jam in the morning, jam at noon,

Bread and jam

By the light of the moon.

Jam . . . is . . . very . . . nice.

When Frances got home, Mother said,

"I have a snack all ready for you."

"I *do* like snacks!" said Frances.

31

"Here it is," said Mother.

"A glass of milk

and some nice bread and jam for you."

"Aren't you worried that maybe

I will get sick and all my teeth

will fall out from eating so much

bread and jam?" asked Frances.

"I don't think that will happen

for quite a while," said Mother.

"So eat it all up and enjoy it."

Frances ate up

most of her bread and jam.

But she did not eat all of it.

After her snack

she went outside to skip rope.

Frances skipped a little more slowly
than she had skipped at noon,
and she sang:

> *Jam for snacks and jam for meals,*
> *I know how a jam jar feels—*
> *FULL . . . OF . . . JAM!*

That evening for dinner
Mother cooked spaghetti and meatball

'I am glad to see there is enough
for seconds," Father said.
"Because spaghetti and meatballs
is one of my favorite dishes."
"Try a little spaghetti, Gloria,"
said Mother.

Frances looked down at her plate.

There was no spaghetti
and meatballs on it.

There was a slice of bread
and a jar of jam.

Frances began to cry.

"My goodness!" said Mother.

"Frances is crying!"

"What is the matter?" asked Father.

Frances sang a little sad song:

> *What I am*
>
> *Is tired of jam.*

"I want spaghetti and meatballs,"
said Frances.

"May I have some, please?"

"I had no idea you liked spaghetti and meatballs!" said Mother.
So Mother gave Frances spaghetti and meatballs, and she ate it all up.

The next day

when the bell rang for lunch,

Albert said, "What do you have today?"

"Well," said Frances,

setting a tiny vase of violets

on her desk, "let me see."

have tomato soup," Frances said.

And a lobster-salad sandwich.

have celery, carrot sticks,

nd black olives.

nd plums, and cherries,

nd vanilla pudding."

That's a good lunch," said Albert.

I think it's nice that there

e all different kinds of lunches

nd breakfasts and dinners and snacks."

So do I," said Frances,

nd she made everything come out even.

The End

43

About Frances

n so glad to see that so many children like
: Frances books, because I had a lot of fun
iting them. I got the idea for the first one,
dtime for Frances, from the little girl next
or who kept finding excuses for not going
bed. After that I began all my titles with B,
r luck. I liked making up the Frances songs.

Here's a little reading song,
Singing it will not take long.
Books are cozy, books are fun.
Now my reading song is done.

ssell Hoban
bruary 2008